CREATURE LOVING VOLUME 5: A MONSTER EROTICA COLLECTION

Lilith Leana

Table of Contents

Acknowledgement

A big thank you to my husband for always believing in me and never making me feel like I couldn't do it.

Cover art

Cover art from Depositphotos

Cover design

Lilith Leana with Canva

Brief Summary

Summoning my Ghost

Camelia summons her late husband each year during the Witching Hour when the veil between the living and the death is the thinnest. This year will be his last visit, so she intends to make the most of their time together.

Samuel spends his time in the spirit world, looking forward to the Witching Hour so he can reunite with his wife again. She doesn't need to say the words, as he already knows this year will be their last. He will show her how much he loves her in their final moment together until they meet again in the next life.

Opera with my Gargoyle

Victoria loves the opera. The music calms her, and the touch of her Gargoyle husband relaxes her even more.

Théo enjoys teasing, and pleasuring his wife during the opera, where she has to remain quiet so they won't get kicked out.

Chased by the Satyr

Each month, Josie eagerly anticipates the thrill of being chased by monsters. This month, she stumbles upon a breathtaking Satyr who captivates her with his irresistible charm and his alluring music.

Sylas lures the sweet Josie to him with the enchanting melody from his flute. The moment she runs, he knows he needs to chase after her, to capture her heart and keep it for eternity. Satyrs do not share.

On a Date with the Yeti

Willa has a crush on a cute, shy Yeti. When he asks her out for a date, she immediately says yes, not realizing that a date with a Yeti is much more than just dining together.

Cole the Yeti has finally mustered up the courage to ask out the human from the shop he visits weekly. Will she become his mate and let him fill her with Yeti babies?

Cooking with the Troll

Amy wants to save her farm by working together with a famous Troll Chef. She didn't expect his hands and ability to create the most amazing flavors with the simplest of ingredients to impress her so much.

Ragnok likes to be alone in his mountain cabin surrounded by pure ingredients to cook with, but when Amy barges in his space, he cannot let her go without having a taste of her first.

On Vacation with the Naga

As Ezra and Nova set off on their first vacation together, Nova quickly learned that the Naga way of vacationing was vastly different from what she was used to as a human.

READER ADVISORY: THIS story contains explicit sex scenes.

Creature Loving Volume 5 is a collection of five previously published standalone short erotic stories and one exciting new bonus story.

It is filled with human FMC's loving Monsters, Beasts and Creatures. Explicit sex scenes, standalone, no cheating or cliffhangers.

Summoning my Ghost

"Trick or treat!" the children yelled as they held out their baskets for candy.

With a smile, I gave them their well-deserved treats on this hallowed Eve. I loved Halloween, and I eagerly watched the hours tick by. With every breath I took, I came closer to the Witching Hour, when the veil between the living and the death was the thinnest.

Each year I had one hour where I could summon my late husband, and we could spend time together. This year would be the last, and I intended to make the most of our short time. I knew the spell by heart and hummed it while I cleaned up the house.

When I saw the last of the children empty the road, returning to their homes to look at the treasures they had received, I locked all my doors and windows. With a happy kick in my step, I went to my bedroom and lit all the candles covering every flat surface. The soft light of the candles made the room bade in a yellow glow, perfect for a meeting between two lovers. I put on my favorite silk chemise, loving the way the soft fabric caressed my naked skin. The heat was turned up, so I wouldn't be chilly under his cold touch.

With closed eyes, I stood in the middle of my casting circle. Salt, crystals, and herbs surrounded me to ward off evil spirits who would want to take advantage of the Witching Hour. As soon as the church bells started to ring and the chimes of my clock sounded, I could feel the cold wash over me. With a smile, I chanted the words that would make my Samuel appear again.

"During this witching hour, I call upon the ancient powers. Spirits of the night let me see, my dearest departed husband before me."

With the last word still hanging in the air, the fire of the candles shivered, and the smell of sulfur filled the room. When the temperature dropped, I opened my eyes, and my husband stood before me.

Samuel opened his arms with a dazzling smile. "My dearest Camelia, it has been too long."

"Only a year, my dear," I said as I stepped into his icy embrace.

I loved the feel of his cold, but solid arms around me. He was becoming clearer by the second, gaining his strength from the spell and my crystals. He cupped my cheek, raising my head so he could study me like he did every year.

"Looking radiant as ever, my love."

I smiled at his endearment and obvious lie. He looked exactly the same as the day he died, only pale, and vaguely translucent. Samuel would never age another day, while my hair was dusted with the gray of my years and wrinkles that no potion or cream could deter covered my face.

"And you're as charming as always," I said. "How is the ghost world?"

"Same old, same old," he said with a shake of his head. "I'd rather know how you are doing."

I updated him about the last year, while safely in his arms. His cold skin cooled mine, but I didn't mind it because I didn't want to spend even one second not connected to him. The moment I had been dreading was closing in on me. After I relayed the latest tale of our grandchild with the corresponding pictures, Samuel captured my chin and tilted my head back up to his. A cold, but gentle kiss grazed my lips, but before I could deepen it, he pulled back.

"What aren't you telling me, Camelia?"

My late husband knew me too well. Twenty years of marriage and twelve visits since his passing would do that to a couple. A sad smile crossed my face, and I knew he understood me without me having to say the words.

"This will be my last visit?" Samuel asked as he caressed my cheek.

I nodded, afraid that my voice would break if I used it now. Another gentle kiss soothed my ache and took my breath away.

"Then let's make sure you'll remember this one until it is time for us to meet again in our next life."

Samuel somehow knew the right things to say at a moment when everything seemed wrong. I nodded and kissed him again. We were done talking for now, and I was ready to feel alive again, even if it would be the last time with him.

His cold and firm lips covered mine. I opened my mouth, licking his lips, coaxing his tongue out to play. He groaned into the kiss and gave me access to his mouth. Our tongues met, and his taste filled my senses. Samuel tasted comforting familiar, like home. I could feel arousal rise inside of me with each sweep of his tongue over mine. He gently eased me down on the bed, breaking our kiss.

"Let me pleasure you, my love. Just enjoy," Samuel said, and let his lips wander lower.

His mouth drifted over my chin, nipping softly to my neck, giving me soft love bites, to my collarbone, laving it with his tongue. Lower and lower he went, goosebumps following the trail off his mouth. He kissed, nipped, and licked every spot he encountered in a leisurely way, as if he had all the time in the world instead of only the fifty minutes that were left in our hour together. Pleasure sparked with each touch of his mouth, and I could feel it burn inside of me.

"Samuel," I moaned, unable to say what I needed, but he knew. He always knew.

"Let me take care of you, my love."

He pushed the soft fabric over my shoulders, exposing my aching breaths to the hot air. It only took a moment before his cold mouth covered one of my nipples, making me gasp from the chilly and wet sensation. The ache in my breasts intensified, focusing on the spot he laved with his tongue. Pleasure radiated from where he was kissing and sucking.

When my nipple felt like a throbbing ice cube, he released it with a plop, and focused on the neglected one. Another gasp escaped me when he gave the other one the exact same treatment, while he gently pinched the first one.

Both of my nipples throbbed with pleasure. The feeling spread across my entire body, although he only focused on one spot at a time. Sparks of pleasure flew from my breasts, as my pussy pulsed, ready to be treated the same way. Arousal already flooded my pussy, and I ached to be filled by my husband.

"I love you," I said, and Samuel smiled in response.

"I know, my heart. Let me show you how much I love you."

Samuel kissed my lips again, slowly, as if time wasn't slipping away. His hands covered my aching breasts, massaging them with his expert moves. The icy touch eased the ache of my nipples, only enhancing my pleasure. His mouth ventured lower again, passing by my breasts, down my stomach to where I was aching the most.

I had forgone panties because I knew how this always played out. Wetness had gathered between my legs, and I opened them when he came close to the spot where I needed him to be. My chemise was gone with a sweep of his hands, and a moment later his cold mouth was on my hot and aching core. He groaned when my taste hit him and lapped my pussy with his tongue like a starved man.

"I survive the spirit world, just for a taste of you each year," Samuel groaned before he dove down again, devouring my pussy.

Pleasure sparked with each sweep of his tongue. He didn't leave any spot untouched. His hands abandoned my breasts to join his mouth between my legs. My nipples were still throbbing with his ministration while his hands discovered new territory. I grasped my nipples, to keep that pleasurable feeling present in my breasts, while he gave me more and more of him. His tongue was lapping at my clit while he entered me with one of his cold fingers.

Samuel always went slowly, prepping me with the utmost care so all I would feel was pleasure. When my pussy was ready, he entered another finger, stretching me carefully. With slow and steady movements he fucked me with his fingers, until my pussy squeezed around him, signaling that I was ready for more. He curled his fingers upwards, seeking out the spot that would make me see stars.

Samuel knew how to play my body like his own personal instrument of pleasure. When he found my G-spot, I let out a choked sound, and he murmured happily. Touching that point while I played with my nipples, and he sucked on my clit, was enough to make the pleasure rise to unseemly heights. It only took a few moments before the pleasure became too much, and I came with a passionate cry.

My whole body trembled while waves of pleasure washed over me. My pussy clenched around his fingers, trying to keep them inside of me while he kept sucking on my throbbing clit. More and more pleasure filled me until it was all I could feel.

I called out his name when it became too much, and he slowly seized his ministrations. Samuel let me come down from my incredible high with gentle movements of his fingers and a soft swipe of his tongue over my clit.

"Hmm, that was-"

"Only the start, my love," Samuel said as he came up for air. "This evening will be all about your pleasure."

"But I want you to join me in it," I said and pulled him on top of me.

"Don't worry, my heart. I take as much pleasure out of seeing you come as I could possibly in this form."

I wrapped my legs around him and grabbed his rock-hard, cold cock with one of my hands. "I want to feel you."

"Everything for you," Samuel said, and in one move he entered me, my wetness easing the way.

My back arched, and an unholy sound came from me when his cold cock filled my hot, pulsing pussy. His body trembled as well, and he closed his eyes, head tilted upward as if in a prayer.

"You feel so alive around me," Samuel groaned.

"Yes," I moaned, as I moved my hips.

With my name on his lips, he started to move inside of me. His icy chest rubbed over my hard nipples, and his cool cock thrust into my pussy. I was hot with passion, while he was cold like the dead, but together we made our love burn like fire.

His cock filled me perfectly, fitting together like two puzzle pieces made for each other. Each thrust made the pleasure rise inside of me, and every sound he made, made my heart grow with love. I memorized every single thing about this moment, wanting to keep it with me forever. His gorgeous face contorted with pleasure, his cold body covering mine, and his cock filling me so perfectly like no other could.

Our sound of pleasure and the harmony of our bodies coming together filled the room. The pleasure inside of me rose, and it wouldn't be long before I would come. I wanted him to join me in the pleasure, so I squeezed my pussy around him.

"Please," I moaned. "Come with me."

Samuel groaned and doubled his effort. His thrusts became harder and faster, pushing me over the edge. With a hoarse scream of pleasure, I came, and Samuel followed me closely behind. My pussy clutched him, and I could feel him pulsating inside of me. Our bodies trembled with our joint release, and our breaths mingled in the kiss we shared. Tremors of pleasure racked my body while his cock throbbed inside me. My body was flush with passion, his cooling me down comfortably.

Samuel stayed inside of me while I came back down from my climax. He looked at me with so much love in his eyes that I could feel my throat sting with emotion. I didn't need to say the words. He could see my own feelings reflected in my eyes.

The passion of our need fueled the kiss we shared. I didn't want to waste any time, and he didn't need any time to recover. He pulled out and rolled me over to my front. With one thrust, he was back inside of me, fucking me again with the same urgency that I felt. Time was slipping away from us, and we needed to make the most of this last moment we had together.

I moaned as Samuel played my body like he owned it. His amazing cold cock fucked me and cooled my overheated pussy. I wasn't sore yet, but I knew I would be after this hour ended. The only upside of having a ghost husband was that he never tired during sex.

This position made him go deeper, giving me more of him. With each thrust he bottomed out, giving me his entire icy erection, and stimulating my clit. He pushed my body into the soft mattress, fucking me with all his strength. All I could do was lay there and enjoy him, moaning in pleasure.

Samuel murmured words of love in my ear, saying how gorgeous I was, how much he loved me, and how good it felt. I savored every word and embraced every thrust.

"Yes, Samuel, my love," I moaned when I could feel my next climax coming closer.

"My heart, my wife, my all," Samuel groaned.

I could feel his cock throb inside of me. My pussy squeezed around him, trying to keep him deep inside, never wanting this moment to end. Almost too soon, pleasure took over, and my next release cascaded over me. Samuel blew a chilly breath in my ear, panting my name while my pussy contracted around him and I moaned back his name. Our names and joined sounds of pleasure filled the room. My body trembled as the pleasure washed over me for the third time in the short time we had together.

Samuel rolled off me with a satisfied grunt. He pulled me into his embrace, face to face. I wrapped my leg around him, cupping his cheek with my hand. He entered me again slowly. Our bodies joined once again, but the urgency was gone. I just wanted to be connected to him, memorizing every inch of his beautiful face.

"Do you want to talk about it?" Samuel asked while his hips moved in a slow dance of seduction.

It was somehow easier to talk about death while connected to my late husband in this intimate way. I nodded, focusing on his eyes while I told him the news that my doctor had told me. His cold embrace grounded me while my voice broke with the news.

"Thank you for sharing," Samuel said as he kissed away the tears that appeared on my cheeks.

"Thank you for listening," I said, because that was all I needed at this moment. There was no fixing this, only acceptance.

"I'm here for you, my love. For whatever you need."

I moved my hips, sparking pleasure again. "I want your pleasure," I said and kissed him.

A low rumble of desire sounded from him as he grabbed my ass, thrusting into me. When he didn't get the right angle to give me pleasure, he rolled us over, pulling me on top. His hands covered my breasts while I sat up and started to ride him. I didn't have as much strength left as I had hoped, but he guided me, helping me with the movement of his hips.

I loved seeing him in the throes of his pleasure, the spark that lit up his eyes shining brighter in the light of the candles. My hands moved over his naked chest, feeling every inch of him I could touch. My gorgeous husband, forever frozen in time.

Samuel thrust upwards, making me lose myself in the pleasure he was giving me. My arms wobbled, and my body threatened to betray itself, but his powerful arms surrounded me. He held me close against his chest, while his hips worked to pleasure me. His cock felt perfect inside of me, his cold body cooling my feverish one.

"I love you," I moaned on his chest, experiencing all the pleasure he could give me.

"I love you too. So, so much, my love. Forever and always in my heart."

Time slipped by while connected to each other. We weren't chasing any high anymore, we just wanted to be together. Pleasure filled my body, making me feel in a perpetual state of ecstasy. When the church bells sounded again, our mouths met. Samuel rolled us over, laying me comfortably on my back while he pleasured me for the last time.

His cock was buried deep inside of me while his hand touched my clit, igniting a final orgasm. His mouth swallowed my cries of pleasure. My entire body was covered by his, trembling with my release, as the pleasure washed over me.

When the last chime struck, and the witching hour was over, my husband disappeared like a dream. I was alone on November first, but I had said my final goodbye, and I was ready for whatever my future would hold, knowing we would meet again in our next life.

THE END

Opera with my Gargoyle

I was sitting in my private box at the opera, waiting for the lights to dim, when I heard him. His heavy footsteps made the ground tremble, and the soft rustling of his wings made goosebumps travel up my arms.

I kept my eyes focused on the stage ahead, but there was no ignoring what his presence did to my body. Every time he entered a room, it was as if my body was ready to receive pleasure from him. My nipples hardened against the soft fabric of my gown and my pussy clenched, producing wetness to ease the way for his massive rock-hard cock.

"Is this seat taken?" he asked.

His rough voice enveloped me like a blanket and made a shiver wash over me. My voice was lost when the music started, so I shook my head. The lights dimmed and suddenly it felt as if we were alone in the world. I sneaked a look at my gorgeous Gargoyle, Théo. His gray skin looked like stone, but I knew it would be soft and cold to the touch. An incredible artist who had made him look like an angel from the heavens carved his face. His big wings and horns gave him a dangerous look, but he was always gentle with me. The ethereal music of the opera filled the room, but I couldn't concentrate on it. My entire being was focused on the Gargoyle next to me, and what his next move would be.

He positioned the chair closer to me and sat down carefully. His massive frame crowded me, and the chair creaked under his weight but held firm. Luckily, the furniture was designed with massive monsters like him in mind. His wings stretched behind him, and the one closest to me grazed my shoulder. The soft texture of his wings caressed me like a lover's touch and made goosebumps travel up my body from the place he touched me.

The first singer appeared on stage and started their part. My Gargoyle rested one hand on my knee, keeping his gaze fixated on the spectacle before us. I tried to focus on the music and listen to the stories the artist was trying to convey, but all I could hear was the blood pounding in my ears, my own breath rising, and his wings rustling behind me.

Ever so slowly, Théo caressed my knee, raising the fabric of my dress higher and higher until his icy hand touched my heated skin. His sharp nails scratched my soft skin, leaving behind thin red lines that only he would see. His hand dipped lower between my legs, and I granted him more access by placing my feet further apart on the carpeted floor.

My hands were resting in my lap, but they itched to touch him. I wanted to pull his hand higher and place it directly on my pussy so he could relieve my ache, but I had to be patient and watch the opera. After what felt like an eternity, his hand moved again. He caressed my naked skin, tracing a path with his claws on the inside of my thighs until it reached the fabric of my panties. His claw scratched over the soft fabric, teasing my already wet pussy.

"I see you are wearing the anniversary gift I gave you, my darling Victoria," his rough voice cut through the music.

Théo always bought me the most luxurious panties to wear, since he was the one who destroyed them every night.

"I love them," I said, hoping he would spare this pair.

With one swipe, he cut a hole in the center of them. With a gasp, I could feel his finger push through the fabric, his claw retracted so he wouldn't harm my delicate skin. The fabric tore to shreds as his hand pushed it away.

"I will be sure to buy you more," my Gargoyle said.

His tail followed the same path as his hand, soothing the scratch his claw had left behind. His finger circled around my pussy, teasing me yet again with a promise of pleasure. My fingers clenched in the bunched-up fabric of my gorgeous dress, needing something to hold on to as he did what he did best. Play me like an instrument of his pleasure.

His finger did a slow dance of seduction over my pussy, sometimes dipping in between my lips to gather my wetness, sometimes circling my clit, but never staying too long in one place. Every move he made was designed to make me painfully aroused, ready to burst at any given moment. His tail hadn't joined in on the fun yet, but I knew it would soon.

"Already so wet for me," Théo said.

He leaned closer to me, applying more pressure on my clit, sparking pleasure inside of me as his tail slid higher. Inch by inch, it came closer to my pussy that was already clenching in anticipation. His breath tickled my ear as his wings surrounded me. I reveled in the masculine, earthy smell that was so uniquely him.

"I want you to come, but not make a sound," Théo whispered in my ear as he circled my clit and his tail entered my pussy slowly.

The music was becoming louder, and the voices of the singers were reaching their heights just as I was reaching mine. As the first act neared its conclusion, I knew he intended to bring me to orgasm before it ended. The pleasure inside of me was building in sync with the music as his hand and tail followed the rhythm. I looked into his stone-gray eyes and nodded. My gaze flicked to his lips as I bit mine. A low growl sounded from him while his eyes focused on my mouth.

"Don't tempt me with that pretty little mouth of yours or I will have to put it to work."

Looking him straight in his eyes, I let my tongue glide over my lower lip, wanting him to lose control. Another growl sounded from him as he increased the pressure on my clit and his tail started fucking me. A gasp escaped me as pleasure sparked, and I knew I was almost there.

His tail was unyielding in its assault on my pussy, diving deeper to find my G-spot. When he touched that magical spot inside of me, I almost shot out of my chair, but his hand held me down. My whole body was trembling with my building orgasm, and I had to bite my lip hard to keep from making any noise. With his finger on my clit and his tail on my G-spot, I wouldn't hold it in much longer.

The singer hit the highest note just as Théo growled, "Now."

Pleasure washed over me as applause flooded the theater. I bit my lip to keep quiet, but I was glad with the sounds surrounding us because there was no way I could keep quiet while pleasure flowed through me. My body trembled as my pussy clenched around his tail and pleasure filled my every sense. My eyes kept locked on his, watching him watch me be consumed by pleasure only enhanced my experience. His cold eyes shot fiery with lust as his finger kept strumming my clit, wringing more pleasure out of me.

His mouth crashed down on mine, devouring me as if I was all he needed in this world to survive. I moaned into the kiss as waves of pleasure washed over me. My hands grabbed his shoulder, loving the feel of his rock-hard body underneath my fingers. Théo was all hard angles and masculine energy, but his hand on me was gentle as he made me come back down from my high.

The lights brightened to a single intermission, and I was happy to have a moment to catch my breath before his onslaught of pleasure would begin again. He offered me his arm as we walked over to the bar for refreshments. Everyone's eyes were on my Gargoyle, but he only had eyes for me. His presence could always control a room, and dressed in a three-piece suit, he was an absolute vision.

I pulled him down by his tie, kissing him and claiming my stake on him in front of everyone. His mouth opened, and I immediately licked his tongue, making the kiss filthy and obscene to look at. When I let him go, he had a dazed look on his face, and his wings surrounded me. His tail caressed my cheek, smelling faintly of me. Before I could do something that would get us kicked out of the opera, he coughed and took a small step back, allowing me to breathe again.

"What was that for?" Théo asked as he grabbed two glasses of champagne from a nearby tray.

"To show everyone that you're mine," I said, accepting the glass he offered.

"All yours, my love. Forever."

I hummed in agreement as I bit my lip, imagining all the things he would do to me when the intermission was over.

After a cool glass of sparkling champagne, he led me back to our private booth. Closing the door with a soft click, we were alone again in our own little bubble of pleasure. He sat in his chair, pulling me in between his legs. His arms and wings surrounded me as his mouth plundered mine. As soon as the lights dimmed again, he gently pushed me down on my knees in front of him.

"Show me that I am yours again," Théo said.

His wings shielded me from prying eyes, but I still felt excitement rush through me as I unbuttoned his pants. His impressive length sprung free from its confinement, and my mouth watered at the sight of him. I never grew tired of seeing his massive ribbed cock in front of me. His veins look like a work of art, carved out of stone with so much attention to detail that it belonged in a museum, but it was all mine.

I locked eyes with him as I stuck out my tongue, slowly licking his head. His earthy taste exploded in my mouth. Mixed with the remnants of the champagne, it was the most delicious thing I had ever had the pleasure of savoring.

"Stop teasing," Théo growled.

His lust-filled gaze and muffled groans only spurred me on. I wanted him to lose control and explode like I had. My hands gripped his rock-hard thighs as I leaned in closer, taking more of his cock in my mouth. I had to open my mouth as wide as I could to be able to fit his impressive girth.

"Fuck, I love your mouth."

With my tongue, I played with the sensitive skin on the underside of his head as my hands moved closer to his length. I could feel his muscles tense as I scratched my nails over his skin. I knew that I had to dig hard for him to be able to feel it. With one hand I grabbed his balls, massaging them as I sucked on his cock.

My other hand circled his length, stroking the part that I couldn't fit in my mouth. I sucked and licked as I stroked his cock, loving the feel of this magnificent creature tremble underneath my hands. I teased the skin underneath his balls, earning a strangled groan from him. After a few minutes of playing, I focused on making him come undone in my mouth. Both my hands grabbed his length and worked him with quick and sure strokes as I sucked on the top of his cock.

Théo looked absolutely magnificent with his head tilted back, biting his lips and his eyes hooded, looking at me as if I was the best thing in the world. I could feel his cock throb in my mouth and I knew it wouldn't be long before he would spray me full of his seed. One of his hands grabbed my hair to hold me steady as his hips worked to push his cock deeper into my mouth. I moaned and opened my mouth wider to take all of him as far as I could.

"I'm going to come," Théo grunted, his hand tightening in my hair.

The sounds he made were like a melody in tune with the music of the opera. A delicious treat just for me. His hips thrust faster as I sucked harder and within moments, he came inside my mouth. I drank down his seed greedily, moaning with pleasure as his body trembled with his release. His hand softened in my hair, and he gently cupped my cheek as I sucked out the last of his delicious seed.

"Show me," Théo growled.

I opened my mouth to show him his seed, and he made a wholly sensual sound, a low rumble of pleasure that I could feel in my core.

"Swallow," he said, and I obeyed his command.

His hand guided me up again while his wings still shielded me from prying eyes. Anyone who would look our way would know that we were doing unholy things in our private box, but they could only guess what kind of depraved acts. His cock was glistening with my saliva, and my pussy clenched around nothing, achingly empty, hungry for his cock.

"I need you," I moaned against his lips.

The music drowned out my words for the audience, but he heard me loud and clear. His mouth covered mine, devouring me like a starved man. Our tongues danced to the rhythm of the music, drinking each other in.

"Take me. I'm all yours," Théo said when I came up for air.

I didn't waste a second and immediately climbed on his lap. Pushing the fabric of my gown away, I grabbed his cock, guiding it between my pussy lips, and slowly sunk down. Each ridge created pleasurable tremors inside of me, making moans slip from my lips. My legs were trembling to hold me steady as I pushed down until he was fully inside of me. A hum of satisfaction left me when I was finally full of my Gargoyle cock that I had been craving all evening.

"So tight and perfect around my cock," Théo sighed in my hair, pulling me close in his embrace.

"So full and hard inside of me," I said. "All mine."

"All yours," he said and started moving inside of me.

His massive hands encompassed my hips, aiding my movement. The sharp sting of his claws piercing the soft fabric of my dress turned me on even more. Nothing mattered at this moment more than our joining.

"Fuck me," I moaned.

"With pleasure," Théo growled.

He grabbed my hips firmly and started fucking me harder. My hands went to his shoulders to keep my balance as he rocked my world in the opera. His movements were leisurely as he took his time with each thrust. Every time he pulled me down on his cock, bottoming out, a spark of pleasure filled me, igniting a fire deep inside of me. My first orgasm of the evening hadn't sated me in the slightest. I craved his cock and his cum inside of me every single moment of every single day.

"I love you," I moaned as the pleasure grew.

"I love you too," Théo growled, his grip tightening on my hips.

He was going to leave more marks that only he would see, and I loved it. I loved him staking his claim on me, as I had done on him.

"More," I moaned, and he instantly knew what I needed.

His tail, which had been dormant for a while, now came out to play as well. It slid up my body over the soft fabric of my dress. It paused at my breasts, circling each of my nipples until they were hard and throbbing, begging to be sucked, but he left them to go higher. His tail reached my mouth, and I sucked the tip, moaning as I could faintly taste myself mixed with his unique aroma. His eyes shot hotter with lust and the pace of his fucking quickened. I moaned around his tail, trying to suck as much of it inside as I could.

When it was nice and wet, he pulled it out, positioning it at my back entrance. He slowly circled my puckered hole, teasing me with the promise of his tail. Théo didn't put it in right away as if was waiting for something. Just when I was about to beg for it, the music reached a high note, and he stuffed it in my ass. The sounds of the music swallowed my moan, and I was grateful for his perfect timing. I loved our nights out at the opera, and it would be a shame if we were to get kicked out for disturbing the show.

My body was humming with pleasure as he started to move. I was double stuffed by my Gargoyle, my pussy and ass full of him and the pleasure rising steadily inside of me. The music was playing as his wings surrounded me, making it feel like a private concert just for the two of us. Our bodies moved to the beat of the drums, coming together in pleasure and lust.

His tail twisted and turned inside my ass, making me gasp with pleasure. His cock moved steadily as his tail did magical things to my ass. There was no way I could be quiet, but luckily the music drowned out the hushed sounds of my pleasure.

My Gargoyle was having a hard time as well. Each time my pussy or ass clamped down on him, he made hungry sounds at the back of his throat. His cock throbbed inside of me as pleasure rose steadily. Every move got me closer to that high just as every note played was going towards the grand finale.

"I'm so close," I moaned against his lips.

"Come for me, my love," Théo growled as his thrusts increased.

After a few more thrusts, I could feel the pleasure rush over me. His hand covered my mouth to keep my sounds of pleasure quiet as my body quivered. My pussy and ass clenched around him, igniting his climax as well. He became feral, fucking me harder, making hungry sounds of desire as his cock throbbed inside of me. My pleasure flowed through me as he filled me with his seed, only enhancing the amazing rush that was going through my body. My pussy milked his cock as he sprayed every last drop inside of me.

"I love our date nights," I said when I was able to speak again.

"Me too." Théo kissed me gently, caressing my quivering body. "Let's go home so I can take care of you."

I nestled closer to him, feeling completely relaxed without a care in the world. He picked me up as if I weighed nothing and took me to our home. Date nights with my Gargoyle husband were the best.

THE END

Chased by the Satyr

Who would chase me tonight? I looked around the Monster mixer to see who would catch my attention, but no one stood out.

Suddenly a melody drifted through the air over the sounds of monsters, and humans chattering. It captivated me in a way that I hadn't experienced before. My legs started walking by themselves and I followed the soft, melodic tones to the edge of the forest where a lone figure stood in the moonlight. His wooden flute produced the alluring tones that captivated me.

He turned around with a smile, and I could see him clearly in the moon's gentle glow. A gorgeous Satyr stood in front of me. His hardened cock jutted out between his muscular goat-like legs. After assessing his impressive equipment, my eyes traveled higher. Coarse, dark brown fur covered his entire body, except the area around his eyes, nose and mouth. The hair on his head was curled and looked softer than on the rest of his body. The curls were adorned with gorgeous curved horns and cute pointy ears. His mouth had a mischievous smile, and when he lifted his flute again, I could see his supple dark red lips touch the tip of it in a sexual move. He was perfect.

"Hi," I said, breaking the sound of his music.

The Satyr pulled away the flute, licked his lips, and smiled. "Hi, to you too."

I motioned to the commotion behind me. "Are you here for the mixer, or are you just wandering the forest, luring a woman to you with your music?"

"Why should it be an or question?" he asked with a wink. "Why can't I do both?"

"True," I said with a nod. "I'm Josie, and you?"

I held out my hand, and he took a step forward to take it. He bowed with a flourish and pressed a delicate kiss on the top of my hand.

"I'm Sylas," he said in his melodic voice.

"Is this your first time at the mixer? I think I would have noticed you before," I asked.

"Yes. Not yours, I take it," he said.

"I've been here a few times already, always with a satisfactory outcome. Do you want to be my partner tonight?"

Sylas took another step closer, towering high over me, and a shiver of anticipation washed over me. His powerful goat-like legs would make him chase after me so fast, that I probably wouldn't even be able to get far ahead. Not that I wanted to run from him for long. I loved the chase and the adrenaline, but I loved being fucked on the ground even more.

The Satyr played with a lock of my hair, winding it around his finger, and tilting my head up. Humming a soft tone, he bent over until our lips touched, and he became silent.

I moaned into the kiss, grabbing his hair to pull him closer. His curls were soft underneath my hands and I tightened my grip. He tasted like the forest, wild and free, and I couldn't get enough of it. His tongue met mine in a fierce dance of passion that ignited a fire deep within me. Arousal coursed through me as our kiss deepened. I wanted him to take me right then and there, but he broke the kiss.

"What are your expectations for this evening?" his melodic voice was serious, and his eyes were searching mine.

I shrugged and smiled up at him. "Whatever you can give me."

His eyes narrowed, and he shook his head. The Satyr touched my chin, lifting my head, making it impossible for me to hide.

"Now the truth, gorgeous."

"The truth," I said.

I searched his eyes, and all I could see was an understanding that I hadn't seen before. He might be able to handle my truth. I took a deep, and steadying breath, and told him what I wanted from him.

"I don't like to run, but I like to struggle. I want you to work for it, to earn the honor of fucking me. I want your hands on me, grabbing me, pining me down while you take me hard. I don't mind bruises, but I don't want you to hurt me. I just want you to grab me, and fuck me hard while I try to get away."

After my confession, I tried to turn away my face, but his hand on my chin kept me in place. His eyes, unlike those of a previous boyfriend, were brimming with desire instead of disgust. Not a lot of people understood my needs, and most were appalled by them, but this Satyr accepted them and had even asked for it.

"It would be my absolute pleasure to chase you," Sylas said and kissed me again.

The kiss turned heated, and I moaned when his tongue met mine in a fiery passion. Our bodies melded together. His rock-hard cock was trapped between us. Before I could grab him, he stepped away breaking our kiss.

"Now, run little faun," Sylas said and he put the flute back at his lips.

A hauntingly quick tone came out of it, making my heart flutter in my chest. I turned around and ran away from the mixer deeper into the woods. I should have probably done all the paperwork and necessary stuff beforehand, but all I cared about now was this Satyr giving me what I craved.

The music followed me into the forest. I couldn't hear his footsteps, only that beautiful tone he produced with his flute. Suddenly, the music was in front of me. I slid to a stop, turned around, and heard the music again. It felt like it was all around me, boxing me in, making me freeze in the middle of the woods.

It slowly died down, and I could hear his footsteps coming closer to me. I ran in the opposite direction, his musical laugh following me. He played the flute again, this time a quicker tone, that rose as fast as my heartbeat. I could hear him following me now, the tone and his footsteps coming closer. My legs trembled as I could feel the adrenaline rush through me. I was ready for him to catch me, and take me.

Suddenly he appeared before me, leaning against a tree. I almost ran into him, stopping just in time. A big grin crossed his face, and I knew mine mirrored it. I turned around, but he grabbed me, pulling me close to him. I struggled, trying to break his grip on my arm, but he was too strong. Arousal and adrenaline coursed through me as he pushed me face-first against the tree.

"All mine now. To do with as I please," Sylas whispered in my ear, his warm breath fanning my face.

I almost moaned at his words, struggling even harder. His whole body pushed mine against the tree, and I could feel his rock-hard erection digging into my ass. I couldn't wait to feel it inside of me, but I wanted more.

"How much do you love this dress?" Sylas asked.

"Not," I said, knowing better than wearing good clothes to the Monthly Monster Mixer.

"Good," he growled, before ripping the fabric apart.

His hands roved over my naked body, while I still struggled to get away. My heart fluttered in my chest as goosebumps traveled across my skin.

"Got some fight left in you, my little faun?" Sylas asked as he backed off.

He put the flute against his lips again, with a twinkle in his eyes, urging me to run. I turned around and ran again, this time naked under the full moon. My pulse quickened with the forbidden longing and the understanding he had of it. I felt free and desired, as I could hear his music float around me. I caught glimpses of the red fabric of my dress as he guided me through the forest. His music led me to an amazing open space in the woods I'd never seen before.

It was almost as if we had crossed a portal into another realm. Thousands of tiny blue flowers covered the open space, illuminated by the light of the moon. The moss on the surrounding trees seemed to glow with an ethereal light. I looked around at the beauty before me as my heart was beating a thousand miles a minute, and suddenly the music stopped. I made a circle, looking for any sign of him, but he was gone.

Before disappointment could rise inside of me, I could feel his hot breath against my neck. "All mine now."

His hand was almost tender on my shoulder until it snaked around my front and took a firm hold of my neck. A moan spilled out of me, as arousal coursed through me. His imposing figure pressed against me, and I could feel the pulsating heat of his desire against my ass.

"No one will hear you scream here, Josie, so let it all out."

The desire to scream rushed through me so I didn't hold back. I screamed at the top of my lungs, the sound vibrating through the forest. Sylas's melodic laugh sounded behind me.

"Good girl. That will be the first of many screams tonight," he said before his hand closed around my throat.

His other hand snaked around my front, pinching my nipple hard, while I struggled in his grip. He was strong and could easily hold me while his hand roved over my body. He dipped lower to in between my legs. A throaty laugh escaped him when he found my sopping wet pussy.

"Already so wet for me, little faun," Sylas said, his warm breath tickling my ear.

One finger slowly entered me, making pleasure pulse in my veins, and a moan erupted from my throat.

"Yes, make me hear your pleasure," Sylas hissed as he circled my clit with his thumb.

I moaned again, louder this time, not holding back the sounds of my pleasure. His cock grew harder behind me as my voice traveled across the open space in the woods.

"Let the forest hear how much pleasure I am giving you," Sylas said.

He pushed another finger inside of me, stretching me with his thick digits. He worked them in slowly, making me used to the invasion as moans kept tumbling out of me. I forgot to struggle. I forgot everything around me as he worked his hand to pleasure me. I could feel the pleasure rise inside of me, ready to burst at any moment, but suddenly he stopped.

"I don't think I've deserved the right to fuck you yet, my little faun," Sylas said, releasing my throat from his hold.

I could still feel his fingers digging into my skin, and I knew that he left a mark around my throat. The pleasure inside of me died down without his ministrations, and I groaned in disappointment. I struggled to get out of his grip, but his powerful body surrounded me.

"Try harder," Sylas hissed.

I struggled harder, suddenly making him release his grip on me. I tumbled to the ground, and in seconds he was on top of me, pushing my face down in the soft green of the meadow. His muscular goat-like legs pinned mine down and his hand grabbed both of mine in a firm hold. I couldn't move an inch, and arousal rushed through me. I was at his mercy, vulnerable, and alone in the middle of the forest, and I loved every second of it.

He moved his legs, pushing mine wide, while still pining me down, and I could feel his cock brush past my ass. I was panting with excitement, so ready for him to fuck me that wetness covered my thighs. My pussy was achingly empty, desperate for his huge cock to fill me.

"Please," I moaned.

"Do you want me to fuck you? Have I earned the right?" Sylas asked as his cock teased my entrance.

"No," I groaned, and I bucked up, trying to throw him off me, but all I did was press my pussy closer to his cock.

A low moan came out of me as I could feel his hot cock head almost penetrate me, but not quite.

"I think I have, little faun," Sylas growled and thrust inside of me in one push.

A scream tore from my throat as his massive cock filled me to the brink. He was big, and throbbing deep inside of me, touching pleasure spots that had never been touched before. This was everything I wanted and needed. His big furry body covered me and pushed me to the ground as his fat cock stretched my pussy.

"Fuck you're tight," Sylas groaned.

He pulled back, and pushed inside of me again, sparking pleasure. I bit my lip to stifle the sound of my pleasure, but somehow he knew.

"Scream for me, Josie. Let the forest hear that I have claimed you," Sylas said.

When he thrust inside of me again, I let the pleasure flow through me, and let the sounds spring free from my throat. I made sounds I've never even heard before as he fucked me on the forest floor. His thrusts became wilder with the more noise I made, so I didn't hold back, and neither did he. The open space echoed with the rhythmic sounds of our bodies colliding and our screams of pleasure.

Our fucking was intense, stoked by carnal ferocity. Each time he pulled back, I pushed my ass up to keep him in my pussy. Every thrust made me see stars, and pleasure burst deep inside of me. His hips slapped against my ass with each pull, and push and his balls hit my pussy.

He touched every pleasure point inside of me, but I knew I needed more. Without me having to say the words, he already knew what I needed. One hand snaked around me, strumming my clit in the same rhythm as his fucking.

Pleasure rose inside of me and suddenly burst. I screamed as my orgasm tore through me, leaving nothing behind but pleasure and lust. My body trembled as my pussy squeezed around his cock, making him go feral. Sylas fucked me even harder, pistoning in and out of my pussy at an unbelievable speed, only prolonging my climax until he came with an earth-trembling roar. His cock pulsed inside of me, giving me all of his seed as the pleasure felt even more intense.

Waves of pleasure washed over me as my whole body felt limp from it. He pulled his cock out and rolled me over. Something in his eyes made a shiver wash over me. He seemed different somehow, more ethereal, as if fucking me had made something snap inside of him.

I crawled back, and his eyes shot hot with lust. In one move he was over me, caging me in. His face was close to mine, and I could smell all of him, a deep green, musky scent that made arousal flood through me. Even though I had just come moments ago, I was ready to be fucked by him again, and again.

"No running anymore, little faun. You're all mine now."

Before I could ask what he meant, his head dove down between my legs. I moaned when his tongue touched my throbbing pussy, lapping up our combined juices. It was filthy and delicious at the same time. He growled with delight as he tongued my pussy. Pleasure flowed through me with each lick, and the sounds that came from my throat didn't sound like me.

"Sylas," I moaned, not sure what I was asking for, but he knew.

"Just let go, Josie," Sylas said before placing his mouth on my clit and sucking.

I screamed out in pleasure as my climax burst through me. Waves of pleasure washed over me as my pussy clenched, and my clit throbbed. Sylas lapped up all of my juices, grunting with pure animal satisfaction. Raw need shot through me as my empty pussy trembled.

"Fuck me, take me, fill me," I moaned as I stretched out my arms to me.

"Yes, beg for it," Sylas said, looming over me. "No more running, or struggling. You're mine now."

He kept saying those words, but before I could confront him about his claim on me, he thrust his enormous cock inside of me. My words caught in my throat as the breath whooshed out of me, and a moan took its place.

"I'm going to fill you with my cum until you're overflowing," Sylas growled while thrusting inside of me.

With his face hidden in the darkness, I could only make out the gleam of his eyes as he leaned over me. An eerie feeling crept over me, as if his words were more than empty promises to arouse me. Realizing he meant it, and that he was staking his claim on me under the full moon, made excitement rush through me.

"Mine," Sylas growled with each thrust.

His cock filled me with pleasure with each pull and push while he kept claiming me with his words and his body. I let him and just enjoyed the ride as pleasure filled my body. I was a slave to the new sensation, open to every new experience. He filled an emotional hunger that I hadn't realized I had until I met him. He understood my needs and gave me my release without judgment.

"Yours," I moaned.

His eyes shot fiery with lust as a feral noise erupted from his throat and he fucked me even harder. I was glad for the soft moss I was lying on as he plowed into me with so much force that my pussy would be shaped for his cock alone. All reason fled me, leaving only the madness of my desire for him. My toes curled, and my back arched from the forest ground as my climax ripped through me. I came in cascading waves of pleasure, my body shaking and my pussy clenching around him.

Sylas groaned, and after a few more thrusts he burst into a bone-deep growl of pleasure. He shot his seed inside of me, my pussy milking him with every last drop. Pleasure filled my every sense as the power of our shared orgasm sent my body into shivering ecstasy.

His movements slowed and he gently pushed some sweaty hair from my forehead. A tender look came over his face as he gazed down at me.

"Mine, forever, little faun," Sylas murmured.

"What do you mean?" I asked when I could breathe again.

"Satyrs are territorial. This pussy is mine now," Sylas said as he pulled his cock out. Cum gushed out of me, and he used his fingers to push it back inside, making me moan. "I will be the one to chase you and fuck you every full moon. It will be my hands that leave marks on your arms when you struggle, and my cock that will claim this pussy over and over again. No other man will ever touch you again."

I moaned at his words, a shiver of delight crossing over my body, and my pussy already clenching, achingly empty. My body seemed to agree with him, my mind just needed to play catch up. But I realized I didn't mind his claim on me. It was refreshing to have someone that would accept every aspect of me, and give me what I needed.

"Kiss me," I said.

"With pleasure," Sylas replied, and dove down for my mouth.

Our lips met, and passion sparked. I could faintly taste myself on his lips, mixed in with his unique aroma. He tasted free like the forest and bitter like dark chocolate, but I loved it. When our kiss ended, we were both panting, and I felt my body ready for another round. He might destroy me, but it would be a worthy way to go.

"I'm yours," I said.

"Mine."

THE END

If you enjoyed this story and want to read more stories about getting Chased by Monsters, check out Chased by the Werewolf[1] and Chased by the Minotaur[2]

On a date with the Yeti

I had a crush on a Yeti. A cute, shy, quiet Yeti.

Every week Cole came down the mountain to get supplies for his village. The Yeti clan owned the surrounding mountains with ski resorts on top of it and were absolutely loaded. But they still came to my little shop for their supplies. Sometimes when there were specific woman needs, it was a human-Yeti couple that came. I loved and hated those days. They were always so kind and showed me pictures of their adorable Yeti babies, but it also meant that I didn't get to see my cute Yeti.

Cole was always so kind and sweet. He let everyone else go before him in line because he knew it took some time to do the checkout with all of his supplies. Despite his massive and frightening appearance, he always wore a gentle smile on his face. He was a man of few words, but he made every single one count.

I was staring out the window during a slow day at the shop when I could see his figure appear over the mountain. My heart started racing, and I looked at the calendar. Cole usually came on Monday, but it was a Friday. Maybe there was an urgent need that he needed to come and get.

I was almost bouncing on my feet by the time he came to my shop, so excited to see him. He entered and went straight to my register.

"Hi, Cole. What can I help you with today?" I asked with a smile, eying the small tree he was holding.

He had pulled it out of the ground, roots and all, and some dirt got on the floor, but it would be easily cleaned up after he left.

"You, Willa," Cole grunted.

"Excuse me?" I asked, not sure if I had heard him correctly.

Cole held out the small tree, and I accepted it, almost caving under the weight.

"Date," he said.

My heart fluttered as I looked at him from over the green bush. "Oh, I would love to. When?" I asked.

"Now," he said and picked me up like I weighed nothing, tree and all.

"Cole, wait," I shrieked. "I need to clean up, and close up my shop."

It was already after three and there was no one around, so it wouldn't be the worst thing to close up early. He nodded and gently put me down.

"How long?" he asked.

I shrugged. "15 minutes."

"I help?" Cole asked.

"Oh, that would be wonderful. Could you maybe plant the tree outside and clean up the dirt on the floor?"

The huge Yeti looked around, only now realizing that he had sprayed dirt all around my shop.

"Sorry," Cole said, letting his head hang down.

I touched his hand and urged him to look at me. "It's okay. It really is a very nice tree, and I would love to have it grow outside of my shop. You meant well, Cole."

He nodded and got to work. With his help, the shop was closed in under 15 minutes and I got dressed for the cold weather, ready for our date. The buzz of excitement coursed through my veins. I always wondered if Cole liked me back because I had seen him sneak looks at me, but he never acted on them. I might be old-fashioned because I still believed that a man should ask out a woman and not the other way around. But if it had lasted any longer, I might have done it.

He led me to the sled he had used to carry the tree with. Soft and cozy fur blankets covered the sled, tempting me to snuggle up.

"You sit, I pull," Cole said.

"Thank you," I said as I sat on the sled.

I admired Cole's strength as he pulled the sled forward as if it was nothing. We both stayed quiet during the trip because I didn't want to yell against the wind, but it was a comfortable silence. We didn't need to talk to enjoy each other's company, and I loved looking at the scenery.

I've lived on this mountain my whole life, but I've never been on the other side of it before. It had always been off-limits and only Yeti territory until a few years ago a woman fell in love with a Yeti and they opened up their clan to outsiders. Business had been booming since they relied on more man-made products than before, and I also had to order baby stuff, which was not cheap.

When we arrived at what seemed to be his home, I was freezing and my teeth were chattering. As soon as Cole picked me up, I instinctively snuggled closer to him, seeking warmth from his body.

"You cold," Cole said almost accusingly.

I chuckled, petting his soft fur. "Yes, I don't have a built-in fur coat like you do."

"You soft," he said as he touched the hair on my head.

"Yes, but I only have hair on my head," I said. Realizing that wasn't true, I could feel a blush rise. "And also somewhere else."

"Where?" he asked.

Cole touched my cheek, almost mesmerized by the heat creeping up. "Between my legs," I said, averting my gaze.

"Can I see?" he asked.

My eyes shot up at him, and I could see lust burn in his. "That depends on how this date goes," I said with a wink.

"I make you warm," he grunted as he brought me inside.

A gasp escaped me when I saw his living space for the first time. It was a small, but beautiful cave. Everything in it was neatly put away, creating a comfortable space to move around in. A massive bed, covered with soft-looking furs, sat against the furthest wall. On the opposite side, there was a small working area to prepare food. In the middle, there was a ring of stones ready for a fire.

The entrance of his cave, carved out from the snow, contrasted with the beautiful stone that composed the interior. Light danced and reflected off the walls, casting an enchanting glow. The sun was going down quickly and the last beams of light illuminated the space.

"Small?" Cole asked, looking at me with worry in his eyes.

"No, it is absolutely perfect," I said with a smile.

Relief flooded his face, and he smiled back at me. "Good. When babies, bigger cave."

I may have ignored the baby's comment because I wasn't ready to get into that conversation yet. Luckily, my growling stomach made for a perfect conversation chance.

"Date, food, drink," Cole muttered as he put me down in front of the fire.

He wrapped a giant fur blanket around me and started the fire. The reflection of the flame against the rocks was gorgeous. I was almost sad that he wanted to swap this cave for a bigger one when the babies came. I got that thought out of my head. This was only the first date. What if he realized he didn't like me at all and dropped me back off at my house and I would never see him again? A shiver went through me at that thought. Cole immediately wrapped another blanket around me and put me closer to the fire.

"Cold?" he asked.

I shook my head with a smile. "No, this is perfect. Thank you, Cole," I said, grabbing his hand before he could leave. "Join me."

He shook his head. "Food, Drink, Date, Breeding," he said almost as if he had made a list of how our date should go.

The low exclamation of the word breeding did some things to my insides that I didn't want to think about.

"Oh, okay," I said, letting his hand go.

Cole went outside and came back with a big pot that he placed on the fire. When he pulled off the lid, I could see a delicious soup floating around in it. He stirred it, and I could already smell all the herbs and vegetables coming together in a delicious aroma.

"Did you make it?" I asked.

He nodded, going back outside and grabbing more stuff. Cole handed me a chilled glass of sparkling wine that I gratefully accepted. He had bought a case of my favorite drink last week, but I hadn't thought too much of it. Now that I knew he was preparing for this date, I felt warm inside. The fire was warming my outside, but his actions were warming my inside.

"Thank you," I said, and he smiled at me.

Cole was gorgeous when he smiled. In an instant, his entire face transformed from monstrous to handsome. I loved looking at his piercing blue, expressive eyes. He might not talk much, but his eyes always conveyed his emotions to me with a single glance.

We ate in a comfortable silence only broken by the sounds of my moans from the delicious food he had prepared. The first moan might have been involuntary, but when I saw how Cole's eyes shot hot with lust, I might have sprinkled in a few more than I would normally.

"Food good?" he asked when I finished my bowl.

"Delicious," I said with a smile, handing it to him.

"More?" Cole asked.

"No, thank you. I'm full," I said.

He nodded and cleaned up the rest of the soup and cutlery. I could see that he was nervous, and I wanted to comfort him.

"Do you want to come sit here, Cole? Enjoy each other's company for a bit," I said, pointing to the seat next to me.

He nodded and came over. When he sat down, I stood up and asked. "Can I sit on your lap? The cold stone is making my butt numb."

Cole acknowledged me with a nod and opened his arms for me. With a happy little sigh, I sat on his lap and laid my head on his chest.

"You're so soft and warm," I murmured as my fingers played with the soft white fur on his chest.

Cole rumbled low, tightening his arms around me. "Good date?" he asked.

I looked up at his gorgeous blue eyes and smiled. "The absolute best, because it is with you. But it isn't over yet, right?"

My sweet Yeti shook his head, his eyes focusing on my lips. I slowly licked my lips, loving the way lust filled his eyes. When I gently bit my bottom lip, a low growl sounded from him. I could feel it vibrating through my body to my core.

"Do you want to kiss me, Cole?" I asked, my voice breathless.

"Yes," he said and dipped his head low until our lips touched.

I moaned into the kiss, having imagined this moment so many times before. Reality definitely won over my imagination. Cole's lips were soft, and hot underneath mine, and when he opened his mouth to let his tongue come out to play, it was like sparks flew. His taste was so pure, and manly, mixed in with the herbs from his soup that I could kiss him forever and never get bored.

He cupped my cheek with his massive hand, angling my head so he could deepen the kiss. My head swam when Cole devoured me with his mouth. Both my hands curled into his fur, needing something to hold on to as my Yeti rocked my world.

The kiss lasted forever, but still not long enough. I broke off the kiss to catch my breath, never letting go of Cole's fur.

"Good kiss?" Cole asked.

"Amazing," I said dreamily, watching his lust-filled gaze.

"Now breeding?" Cole asked as his hands tightened around my waist.

"Maybe a bit more foreplay first?" I asked.

I let my hands wander lower over his chest to his covered erection. It was straining against the fabric, desperate to break free. With a groan, Cole ripped off his shorts, his cock springing free from its confinement. My mouth went dry when I had the first look at his magnificent equipment.

It was massive, pink and hard. My hand closed around it, and I could feel it throb underneath my touch. Cole groaned low as I could see a drop of precum pearl on the tip. I slid off his lap and kneeled in between his knees.

"Can I taste you?" I asked.

A low rumble sounded from his chest as he nodded. I teased him a bit by licking my lips again, while his piercing blue eyes remained focused on me. He pushed his hips up slightly, making his cock sway in front of my eyes. I couldn't resist it any longer and grabbed it with both my hands. Without wasting another second, I put my mouth on the tip, licking off the drop of precum. I moaned as his taste exploded in my mouth, a musky, manly mix I could get addicted to.

"Willa," Cole groaned my name.

I let his head go with a plop and smiled up at him. "Yes, Cole."

"Don't stop," he said as he gently pushed my head down again.

I took his cock back in my mouth, sucking on it as I caressed him with my hands. He trembled under my touch as his hand gently brushed away the hair from my face. The sounds he made, and the way he looked at me, made arousal rise inside of me as well. I could feel wetness seep into my panties as I licked his cock, imagining how it would fit inside of me.

I had played with the idea of dating him for a long time, so I had ordered some large dildos to prepare myself, but Cole was of another caliber altogether. My fingers could hardly touch each other when I grabbed him with both my hands.

I knew I had to get him and me nice and wet before it would ever fit. I gave him one last suck before licking him from top to bottom. The groan he let out made my insides quiver. My pussy was achingly empty, and I needed him inside of me.

I stood up, giving him the most seductive smile that I could as I unbuttoned my shirt.

"If I had known we were going on a date, I would have worn something more sexy today," I said, looking at my day-to-day clothes.

"Willa always sexy," Cole growled, grabbing my hips and pulling me closer to him.

"You too," I gasped as he ripped the shirt open in one move.

Buttons scattered around the cave, but the appreciative groan when he saw my black bra was worth the ruined shirt. I quickly shimmied out of my jeans before he would tear those two. My panties and bra followed, and I stood naked before my very aroused Yeti.

"Bed?" Cole asked.

"No," I said, climbing on his lap. "I want you here, like this, now. I've waited for you to ask me out for so long, and I cannot wait another minute to have your cock inside of me."

Cole growled low as I pushed my pussy against his cock, coating it in my juices.

"You like me too?" he asked.

"So much. Otherwise, I wouldn't be here, and I wouldn't be so wet." I grabbed his hand, letting him feel how aroused he made me. "This is all because of you."

Cole growled my name again, the sound vibrating through me and only making me wetter. I grabbed his cock with one hand, aiming it at my entrance, and let myself sink down on it. Our pleasured exclamations sounded through the small cave as his enormous cock filled my pussy. It was a tight fit and my pussy felt like it was being stretched to its limits, but he fit inside of me. Slowly I sunk down, lower and lower, until the entirety of his length was inside of me.

"Tight," Cole growled as his eyes closed.

I gasped when he filled me like no man had ever done before. His cock touched every pleasure point in my pussy and I could feel the pleasure rush through me. My legs trembled, but his powerful hands held me steady.

"Fuck me," I moaned, unable to move myself. "Breed me. Make me yours, Cole."

"Mine," he growled low before his hands tightened around my hips and he lifted me up and dropped me down again.

"Yes, all yours," I moaned as pleasure filled my senses.

I knew Yetis mated for life, and I couldn't imagine anyone else to spend the rest of my life with. Cole was perfect for me. Sweet, kind, and gentle, and his amazing cock was rocking my world right now.

His pace quickened and soon he was using me as a fuck-doll for his own personal pleasure, pistoning me on top of his cock. I enjoyed the ride, making all kinds of sounds I'd never made before. His growls of pleasure only enhanced mine, and the look of absolute bliss on his face pushed me over the edge. I screamed his name as pleasure washed over me. My pussy clenched around his cock, igniting his own orgasm as well.

He growled low, fucking me a few more times on his cock before he filled me with his cum. I moaned when his warm seed filled me until it overflowed, leaking out of my pussy and making a mess. His arms embraced me, cradling me against his chest, and I sighed, loving the warm and soft feel of his fur against my naked skin.

"Bed," Cole said as he picked me up as if I weighed nothing.

His cock was still inside of me and I gasp when it pushed against my G-spot. It hadn't softened yet, and my pussy was greedy for more of his cum. My muscles squeezed around him and he growled low.

"Not done yet," Cole growled.

I wasn't finished with him either, but my aching muscles disagreed. He laid me on the soft furs of his bed and I stretched my arms to caress the amazing textures. He pulled out, leaving me achingly empty, making me moan with the loss.

His burning eyes on me made me feel better. He devoured me with his gaze, taking in every naked inch of my skin. I was usually self-conscious about being naked in front of a date, but with Cole, it felt natural. I arched my back off the bed, pushing my breasts up. My nipples hardened when a cold gust of wind entered the cave. Goosebumps traveled up my arms as a shiver washed over me. Cole immediately covered me with a heavy fur and went to the fire to stoke it higher.

"Cold," he said.

"I won't be if you joined me between the furs," I said, my voice hoarse from all my screams of pleasure.

"Yes," he growled and came over.

I pushed the fur down, exposing my breasts. "I think you can warm up my breasts with your hot mouth," I said.

He climbed on the bed, caging me in with his massive body. My nipples were hard and aching, begging for his attention. He touched one nipple with his big finger, caressing it gently until I moaned with pleasure.

"Soft," Cole growled before he bent down and put his mouth on my breast.

I gasped, grabbing his hair as his tongue laved over my nipple, making sparks of pleasure ignite inside of me. He circled my nipple with his tongue, slowly looking at me to see my reaction. I loved the feel of his soft hair running through my fingers as his tongue did magical things to my body. He switched breasts, giving the same attention to the other one as the first one became exposed to the cold air, making it pucker even more because of the wetness of his saliva.

"Oh Cole, that feels so good," I moaned.

"Delicious," he growled as he let my nipple go after a last lingering lick.

"Please, don't stop," I said, grabbing his hair tighter so he couldn't pull back too far.

"Never," my Yeti said, our eyes locked and the emotions I could see in them almost made me choke up.

I suddenly realized how much this date meant for him. He might not have the right words to tell me, but he showed me with his actions and I could see how he felt in his eyes.

I cupped his cheek and let my thumb glide over his lips. His tongue flicked out, licking my thumb and I moaned, loving that soft wet texture on my naked skin.

"Never," I said, knowing that one word encompassed so much.

"Mine," he growled.

"Yes, and you're mine," I growled back, tightening the grip I had on his hair.

I would not share my perfect, shy Yeti with anyone. This might only be the first date, but I knew this was it and I knew Yetis mated for life.

"Fuck me, Cole. Fill me with your cum and breed me."

He growled low, my words lighting a fire inside of his. "Knees."

As I turned around, dropping to my knees, he wasted no time in grabbing my waist and pulling me back, pressing my face down. In one move, he was inside of me, filling me with his amazing cock. I moaned when it felt like he went on forever. He could get even deeper in this position, giving me every inch of his delicious cock.

Sounds I didn't even recognize as my own left my mouth as the tip of his cock hit my G-spot.

"Yes, Cole," I screamed. "That's the spot."

With an earth-trembling growl, he started fucking me hard. If his hands hadn't held me steady, I might have shot off the bed from the force of his thrusts. With every single thrust, he hit my G-spot, making me see stars. Pleasure filled my every sense and in no time at all, I could feel my orgasm rise inside of me.

If sex with Cole would be like this every time, I would be one happy wife. It was as if his cock was made for my pussy, fitting me perfectly, so I had to stretch to accommodate his girth, but not too big that it hurt. His cock touched every pleasure point inside of me with every thrust. Moans fell from my lips as pleasure rose inside of me. It only took a few more thrusts before it became too much and I burst.

My pussy squeezed around him as my body trembled and my toes curled. Pleasure washed over me in waves, the groans from Cole only enhancing my bliss. His hands tightened around my hips, fucking me harder until he came as well, filling my pussy with his seed. I could feel his cock throb deep inside me as my quivering pussy milked out the last of his cum.

With a sigh, I let myself fall on the sheets, my heart fluttering in my chest and my body still shivering with pleasure. He slowly pulled out, grabbing a towel to clean up the mess we had made.

"So, how is this going to work?" I asked when I could catch my breath and I was safe and warm in the arms of Cole.

"Willa, mine," he said, and his embrace tightened around me.

I chuckled, patting him on the arm. "Yes, we've established that. I still need to run my shop."

"Day shop, night here," Cole said.

"Okay, and what will you do?"

"Help you," my sweet Yeti said.

"It would be nice to have some strong hands around," I said, nestling closer to him.

This first date turned out better than I could have hoped.

THE END

If you enjoyed this story and want to read about more Yetis breeding their mates check out:

Saved by the Yeti[1] and Trapped with the Yeti[2] and Waking the Yeti[3].

---

1. https://books2read.com/u/bQj7VP

2. https://books2read.com/u/bopvPZ

3. https://books2read.com/u/bxNkYD

Cooking with the Troll

I hated Chefs. Especially self-entitled, secluded living, mountain Troll Chefs. Or at least this one in particular. But I really needed this contract, so here I was, trotting up a stupid mountain in search of the Chef who lived there.

It might have been a pleasant walk if I hadn't had to pull my cart full of vegetables. I was a sweaty mess by the time I reached his dwelling. Why could he not have a road paved up to his house? Did he not want any visitors?

I took a moment to catch my breath before ringing the bell, not wanting to be out of breath when meeting the Chef for the first time. I had heard many tales about the famous Troll Chef who had opened numerous well-running restaurants. Everything he touched seemed to turn to gold, and I needed a piece of that to keep my farm running. His latest venture would be a vegetarian restaurant in the city from only locally sourced ingredients.

Despite having the smallest farm in the area, mine was the most diverse. I planted almost every seasonable vegetable that I loved, caring for it as if it were my own children. I knew it would be smarter to focus on one type and go big, but I just could never choose. Luckily, this had made me the number one pick for his venture. He just needed to approve of my produce and we could sign the contract that would save my farm.

When the door opened, I had to take a step back to take in the entirety of the male standing before me. He was massive, shaped like a bolder, and his skin had the same color as the mountains surrounding us. A black chef's jacket covered his bulging arms, and simple jeans covered his trunk legs. His face was wide and in the middle sat a broad nose that suited him well. He had to duck to get through the door so his horns wouldn't catch in the door frame. His black hair stood upright as if he put his hand through every time he was annoyed, which according to the look on his face now, was probably a lot.

He was far from handsome, but there was something about him that attracted me to him. I just couldn't put my finger on it. The Troll eyed me with suspicion until he saw the cart with vegetables I had pulled up the mountain. He almost pushed me aside to get a look at all my produce.

"You the farmer?" he asked, his voice gravely like two rocks grounding together.

"I wouldn't have hoisted all of this with me if I wasn't," I bit out.

He nodded, ignoring my irritated tone, and turned around. "Follow me."

"Yes, Chef," I muttered.

He turned around again, and I almost bumped into him. He was towering over me. I was a big girl; I had to run a farm by myself, but next to him, I felt small and dainty.

"Say that again," he growled.

"Yes, Chef?" I said, not sure what he wanted from me.

"Don't ask it. Say it," he said and his voice unlocked something inside of me.

I was not getting aroused by the man who could change the future of my farm, but I did open my mouth to obey him.

"Yes, Chef," I said, my voice firm with just a hint of huskiness that came from my clenching core.

He opened his mouth as if to say something, but seemed to change his mind. He grabbed the handle of my cart and pulled it into the house. I gasped when we entered the kitchen. From the outside, the mountain cabin had looked small and almost unassuming, but the kitchen was a real masterpiece.

I wasn't the greatest cook, but this kitchen would inspire me to try. It had all the latest technology and appliances, but it was all covered in wood, giving it a cozy vibe. He had miles of counter surface, three ovens, and the biggest stove I had ever seen. Without counting, I assumed it had at least a dozen fires. In the middle was a massive kitchen island that could seat at least ten people on one side.

He put the cart on the kitchen counter with no effort at all. Picking up each produce one by one, he inspected and sniffed them. I appreciated someone being thorough and looking at the quality of my vegetables. When he unloaded the cart, he put it by the door.

"So, what do you think? Good enough for your restaurant?" I asked.

"I will need to cook with them first."

That was fair and expected for such a big contract. I wasn't too nervous because I knew my vegetables were of top quality. Most of the hassle had been delivering them here.

"Okay, when do you think I can come back for a definitive answer?"

"If you stay, you will have it by this evening. And you will know what I will make with them."

"Okay, no problem," I said with a smile.

The sooner I had my answer, the faster I could relax again. He slid a chopping board my way and nodded at the potatoes. "Clean those."

"So you expect me to deliver the ingredients and do all the hard work?" I asked, quirking an eyebrow.

"The faster those potatoes are peeled, the quicker I can prepare the rest of the food. As a farmer, I can imagine you know how to use one of these?" he asked as he put a knife in front of me.

"The farmer has a name," I muttered as I grabbed the knife, contemplating sticking it in his gut for only a moment before I focused on the potatoes.

"And that name is?" he asked.

"Amy. And yours?"

"My name is Ragnok, but in the kitchen, you will address me as Chef."

I rolled my eyes but didn't want to argue, so I just focused on my potatoes. I loved the smell of fresh vegetables and potatoes were no exception.

We worked in an almost comfortable silence. Every once in a while, he slid a new vegetable to me and said how they should be cut, but apart from those sparse few words, he was quiet.

His hand might have lingered a bit too long when he handed me a vegetable and I could swear I felt his eyes on me whenever I wasn't looking at him, but I tried to ignore it. It would not be professional to develop a crush on the Troll that could help save my business.

It was great to see someone operate in their environment. Ragnok was a massive Troll, but he whooshed around in the kitchen as if he were floating. It was like he did ten things at the same time, creating scents that made my stomach rumble.

The hours flew by without me even noticing, and in no time, he started plating. I almost drooled at how effortlessly he placed each ingredient. The fact that he had rolled up his sleeves and his massive forearms were flexing with each move might have something to do with it, but I would never admit it.

"Do you want a taste?" Ragnok asked when he saw me look at the plate in envy.

"I would love to," I said.

I could not imagine working hours on something and not even being able to enjoy it myself.

"Yes?" Ragnok asked, lifting his eyebrow up.

I rolled my eyes and sighed. I knew what he wanted from me.

"Yes, Chef," I said.

Ragnok nodded with a low rumble and put a plate in front of me. His massive body was so close to me that I could feel his body heat warm me. My pussy was pulsing, eager for attention. I ignored it, trying to focus on what he did with the food.

Ingredient after ingredient was joined on the plate until it was a beautiful picture, almost too pretty to eat, but I had been working for hours and only had a sandwich for lunch, so I dove in.

I always thought that people moaning over food were doing it for attention, but I could not hold back the moan of delight that erupted from my throat as I tasted his food. It was so good that I could even ignore the smug look on his face as I devoured every bite. I could have never imagined this from the simple ingredients I had brought with me. He was clearly a master of his trade and if he wasn't so annoying I would have even complimented him.

Without a word, he presented me with the next dish. Why did he have to be so close for the plating, and why was I getting aroused by seeing his skillful hands at work? I crossed my legs to try to ignore the throbbing of my pussy and focused on the food in front of me.

Ragnok presented me with dish after dish that blew my mind and did things to my mouth I would never recover from. The final dish was the dessert. I was never one for sweet things, and I didn't want to lose the taste of all the amazing things he had created with something overly sweet, but he presented me with a simple-looking mousse. I hadn't seen which ingredients he had used for it, so I was curious.

The first bite was like an orgasm on my tongue. Sweet, savory, and spicy were mixed together in a dance that I could almost see if I closed my eyes.

"What is this?" I asked.

"Eggplant, black chocolate, and chili," Ragnok said with a smile.

"It's delicious," I said, taking another bite and moaning at the feast in my mouth.

"You know what would make this taste even better?" Ragnok asked, taking a step closer until he was hovering over me.

I shook my head, not even able to imagine anything better than this.

"Just a dash of your arousal," he said, his voice low and husky.

I gasped. How had he known I had gotten aroused during this little taste fest? My panties were drenched, and I clenched my thighs together to lessen the ache.

Ragnok moved closer, slowly, as if not to spook me, but I couldn't move even if I wanted to. I was completely entranced by this big Troll and his magic in the kitchen. How could anyone create such a feast with only the simplest of ingredients?

His enormous body caged me against the kitchen counter. He turned the bar stool around so I was face to chest with him and the mousse behind me was almost forgotten. I had to crane my neck to be able to look into his eyes, and the lust I could see in them made me gasp again.

He lifted his hands and licked his index finger. His other hand opened my jeans, pulling down the fabric of my panties and exposing my pussy. I moaned when he pushed his wet finger in between my pussy lips, gathering my arousal. Pleasure rose with the movement of his finger. Too soon, he pulled his hand back. His finger was glistening with my arousal, the scent heavy in the air.

Ragnok sniffed it with a groan. "Perfection."

My pussy clenched, producing even more wetness for him to use. He dipped his finger in the mousse, presenting it to me. I opened my mouth and licked his finger, moaning when the taste exploded in my mouth. It was indeed perfection. The sweet and spiciness of the mousse, mixed with the tanginess of my arousal and the saltiness of his skin. Nothing could ever top this. He had ruined me for any other dessert in the world.

"My turn," Ragnok said, and before I could react he scooped up some of the mousse and slathered it over my pussy.

I moaned when the cold texture hit my heated pussy, but he immediately licked it all up with his hot tongue. He pulled down my jeans and panties until

I was naked waist down on the bar stool. I grabbed his horns to keep steady as his massive tongue licked every inch of my pussy. He took his time, teasing and tasting me as if he was planning a six-course meal with my pussy as the main ingredient.

I moaned, pushing my hips up to get more of his tongue, but his low and throaty chuckle made me realize he was testing me.

"Please, Chef," I moaned.

Ragnok growled low, those two words making something ignite inside of him, and he devoured me. His massive tongue zeroed in on my clit, and sparks of pleasure burst inside of me. His hand tightened around my legs, keeping me spread wide so he could eat me out better. Moans, and gasps left me as he licked me everywhere.

He curled up his massive tongue and pushed it inside of me, making me scream with pleasure. My pussy clenched around his tongue as my body trembled. My orgasm was rising with each lick, flick, and push of his delicious tongue.

"Oh, I'm going to come," I moaned.

Ragnok growled low against my pussy, making vibrations go through me and only enhancing my pleasure.

"Yes, Chef. Please, Chef," I moaned.

He doubled his efforts, thrusting his tongue in and out of me, fucking me with his delicious wet appendage. My pussy clenched as pleasure rose and when he pulled out, focusing on my clit, I burst. I screamed as pleasure washed over me, my clit throbbing as he flicked over it with his tongue. My body trembled as my pussy clenched, producing even more wetness that he happily lapped up.

Ragnok didn't want to let any drop go to waste as he licked me gently, coaxing more pleasure out of me. When he sat up, his lips shining with my juices, he licked them off slowly, showing the delicious tongue he had used so amazingly.

Catching my breath, I chuckled. "I hope you're not going to serve that at your restaurant because I don't think I can deliver that on a daily basis."

He shook his head, placing soft kisses on my thighs where his fingers had gripped me tight. "That was only for you and me, Amy. I don't like to share."

A shiver went down my spine when he said my name all gravely and sexy like that.

"Yes, Chef," I said.

He picked me up as if I weighed nothing. On instinct, I wrapped my legs around him, feeling the press of his rock-hard erection against my pussy.

"In the bedroom, you can choose what you call me, as long as you scream it with pleasure when you come," Ragnok said.

"Hmm, yes, Chef," I said.

"You have no idea what you do to me when you say those words. I've never been hard plating a dish before, but those words from those pretty little lips and I cannot help myself," he growled before his mouth slanted over mine.

I moaned into the kiss, loving the taste of his mousse mixed with my juices balanced out by his unique, musky taste.

Ragnok let me fall on the biggest bed I've ever seen. Before I could take in my surroundings, he ripped off his chef's jacket, giving me a full view of his broad chest. My pussy clenched when he pulled down his pants and his massive cock sprang free. It was a tint darker than his skin, with a mushroomed head and I could see the veins running across his length throbbing with need. My mouth watered, dying to taste him, but my pussy needed him more.

Before my brain would be too focused on all of his deliciousness, I had to know about the contract.

"Wait, before we go any further. I need to know that this has nothing to do with the delivery contract and that we can separate business and pleasure. I don't want to earn a contract on my back," I said, holding up my hand.

"Yes. The contract was yours the moment I smelled your produce," Ragnok said.

When I quirked an eyebrow, he chuckled. "Your actual vegetables. Your farm is the best fit for the restaurant and I already knew that before I even saw your vegetables. The fact that your smell made me crazy and your taste has me wanting more has nothing to do with that."

"Okay, then fuck me with that big cock of yours, Chef Ragnok."

"With pleasure," he growled, crawling on the bed.

His massive frame dipped the mattress, making me glide towards him. He grabbed my legs and pulled me closer until his cock was flush against my pussy. I moaned at the skin-to-skin contact, craving his length to fill my emptiness.

I might have a thing for Chefs, I realized as I watched the fire in his eyes ignite when I uttered those two words again. "Yes, Chef."

Ragnok pushed his cock in between my pussy lips, coating himself in my wetness. He was massive, but I knew I could take him and I craved his gigantic cock inside of me.

"Stop teasing," I gritted out between my teeth.

"But I love it when you beg, Amy," Ragnok said with a wink.

I gripped his cock, squeezing his throbbing flesh until he moaned. It felt like hot stones covered in velvet underneath my hand, and I couldn't wait to feel it inside of me. His veins were like hard ridges underneath my fingers.

"Let's see who will beg for it," I said. "Now fuck me, Chef."

"Fuck, you're marvelous," Ragnok said before he pushed his cock against my entrance.

"Yes, Chef," I said before a moan took over my words.

I moaned when his giant cock stretched my pussy as he entered me slowly. He was so hot and so big it felt like nothing I'd ever experienced before. It was almost as if I was burning up inside in the best way possible.

"Fuck, you feel amazing," Ragnok groaned.

"Yes, Chef. Now move," I moaned.

"Yes, Amy," Ragnok said with a wink and pulled back.

I moaned when the ridges of his cock touched every point inside my pussy as he pulled back. When he pushed in, even more pleasure sparked. My pussy clenched around him as if wanting to keep him inside.

"If I could plate the feel of your pussy, I would be one rich Troll," Ragnok growled low.

He pulled back again, fucking me hard into the mattress. My hands grabbed his shoulders, loving the feel of his rock-hard muscles underneath my fingers. Pleasure sparked with each thrust and moans tumbled out of my mouth of their own accord.

His groans of pleasure only enhanced my own. His cock throbbed inside of me, and I knew he wouldn't last much longer. I pushed a hand between us, reaching for my clit. Ragnok lifted his hips up, grabbing my legs and pulling them high up on his chest so I could reach my clit better and his cock came even deeper.

He hit a spot deep inside of me that almost made me see double. A few more thrusts and my orgasm washed over me and pleasure like I've never experienced before filled my senses. My pussy squeezed around his cock, and he grunted, coming as well.

Ragnok filled me with his hot cum, making my pleasure only more glorious. Sounds I've never heard before left me as my climax burst into a million pieces. My body trembled as my pussy milked the last of his release.

Ragnok pulled out of me, letting himself fall on the bed next to me. Catching my breath, I snuggled closer to him, happy when his arms circled around me. I was glad he was a cuddler. I really needed some skin-to-skin contact after sex.

"Stay the night," Ragnok mumbled in my hair.

"Yes, Chef," I said and smiled when he rumbled low.

The trip up the mountain had definitely been worth it.

THE END

Bonus Story: On vacation with the Naga

I've been dating Ezra for a few years, but somehow we've never been on a vacation to a Naga resort together.

He had warned me and told me everything I could expect, but nothing could have prepared me for the amount of naked people I saw the moment we stepped off the boat. Everywhere I looked, I could see naked bodies, about half of which were fucking.

I followed Ezra as I felt like I didn't have enough eyes to see everything around me. Arousal was coursing through me as the sounds of sex surrounded us. He checked us in, grabbed my hand and our suitcase, and led us to our room. As soon as the door closed, I felt like I could breathe again.

Ezra looked at me with concern. "Are you sure you're okay with this?"

I bent over, breathing fast, and held up a hand. "Yes, I just need a second to process."

Ezra held my hand patiently, waiting for my breathing to turn back to normal.

"We can always go back home," Ezra said.

I shook my head and stood upright again. "No. I love it. I am so aroused right now, but it was just a lot to take in," I said, holding his hand tight and looking at him. "Let's just go over our ground rules again."

Ezra nodded and cupped my cheek. "All I want is you, Avery."

"And I you, but sometimes I fear I might not be enough for you." I waved my hand around. "I can't be three different types of creatures or..."

With a kiss, he cut off whatever foolish thing I was going to say next. "I love you, I choose you, I want to be with you," Ezra said, pulling me close to him. "I enjoy watching, but I enjoy watching you even more. I want you to be the one that is in my arms each night and that I get to fuck, no one else."

His soft words made something warm inside of me and I couldn't hold back the smile that curved my lips. "I love you too."

"So, do you want to get naked and go to the beach to fuck each other's brains out?" Ezra asked with a wink.

"Yes," I said with a laugh.

We took off our clothes, and I packed a beach bag with the necessary stuff. Even though we didn't bring a lot of clothes, my suitcase was still full of cremes, sunglasses, books and games. Ezra had laughed when he saw how many books I had packed, but my idea of a perfect vacation was reading and fucking him.

He handed me a yellow bracelet with our room number on it. "This is like with the wedding," I said.

Ezra nodded. "The color shows the interest in participation or not, and with the room number, we can get all our bills in the right place. Some people don't even pack a bag when coming here."

"Some people might not need a five-step skincare routine," I said, giving him a shove.

His scales always looked perfect. He just needed to take a shower and go to a descaling spa every few months and he was good to go. Humans had it harder with our sensitive skin.

"Let's go. I can't wait to rub you in with your sun lotion," Ezra said as he pulled me against his body.

"Sunscreen," I said.

"Doesn't matter. As long as I get to rub it all over you," he said.

We went to the beach and Ezra's hands and tail didn't leave me for a second. I was already wet and ready for him. He could take me right here and now, and I wouldn't even protest, but I also wanted to see the beach.

We arrived at two signs. One sign showed a naked Naga sunbathing, and the other showed naked Naga's fucking.

"Which one do you want to try?" Ezra asked me.

I looked at him with a sultry smile. "I really, really want you to fuck me on the beach," I said.

His tail slipped between my butt cheeks as he stepped closer. "Let's go to the beach then," he hissed.

Arousal coursed through me as I saw Naga, humans, and monsters of all kinds fucking each other. The sunlight reflected off the horn of a Minotaur as he plowed into a Naga female, who was screaming with pleasure.

Ezra rolled out our towels as I looked around, trying to take everything in. He picked up the sunscreen and directed me on the towel.

"First things first," he said with a wink as he splashed a generous dollop of sunscreen in his hand. "I've been waiting to rub you all over since we stepped off that boat."

I stretched my arms above me, pushing my breasts higher. "We wouldn't want me getting burned," I said.

Also seriously because I had way too pale skin to just lie on this beach like he could. I loved that Ezra remembered those little things about me and didn't find it annoying that I had human skin that burned easily instead of sturdy scales that could protect me.

Ezra rubbed his hands together to warm up the cream before covering my breasts with both of his hands. I moaned at the contact, my nipples immediately hardening under his touch. He rubbed in the lotion with great care so as to not miss a single spot.

Arousal rose with each caress, only enhanced by the sounds of pleasure around me. I needed him to fuck me, but I also needed him to finish rubbing the sunscreen on my skin. But that didn't mean I couldn't tease him a bit.

As he focused on my breasts, I opened my legs and moaned. "I'm so empty."

I could see his rock-hard cocks sway with every movement he made. Wetness gathered between my legs as I focused my eyes on his cocks, licking my lips.

Ezra groaned as his movements faltered. "I'm almost ready with your front. Do not distract me."

When he applied the rest of the sunscreen, he motioned me to roll on my front. I moved to my hands and knees, pushing my ass backward with my legs open wide. I knew that he could smell my arousal, but my thoughtful boyfriend first applied the sunscreen on my shoulders and back.

Only when he was satisfied that I was sufficiently covered in the cream, did he grab my legs and open me wide. Before I could say another word, his tongues were in my ass, and pussy and pleasure shot through me.

"Yes, Ezra," I moaned as he tongued me in all the right places.

His hands tightened around my legs as his tail slipped around to my front. As he stuffed my ass and pussy with his tongue, he circled my clit with the tip of his tail, making me moan with pleasure. I didn't care about the sounds I made or how I looked. All I cared about was the pleasure only Ezra could give me.

"Please, Ezra, fuck me," I moaned.

"Fuck, I love to hear you beg," he hissed.

After one last lingering lick, he slithered higher over my body. I loved feeling his scales brush over my soft skin. His mouth was at my ear, and I could feel his warm breath brush past my cheek.

"Do you want my cocks?" Ezra asked as I could feel them poke me in the ass.

"Yes, please."

"Where do you want them?" Ezra asked, already knowing the answer.

He had prepped my asshole with his tongue, and I felt achingly empty in both my holes in a way that only he could cure. I whined, pushing my ass closer to him, but his hands on my hips stopped me.

"I want to hear you say it," Ezra hissed.

A shiver washed over me as his voice turned hoarser. "I want you in my ass and pussy," I said.

He hummed, satisfied with my answer. With a gentle caress, he flicked his tongue against my cheek as he pulled back, positioning his cocks. He angled my hips so he could see my pussy and ass. I let my cheek rest on the towel, looking at the ocean in front of me as my boyfriend slowly pushed inside of my pussy. A sigh of satisfaction left my lips as his bottom cock filled my pussy. When he was halfway inside, he pushed his top cock against my asshole.

Ezra groaned when he breached my hole. "Fuck, I love how tight you are for me. Always so ready for both my cocks."

I moaned in response, not able to say a sensible word as he filled both my holes with his amazing cocks. He slowly pushed until he was fully inside, giving me a moment to get used to him filling me. We've had sex more times than I could count, but every single time it felt like he gave me all of him.

When I was ready, I moaned, pushing my hips backward. He hissed as he pulled back and pushed inside of me again, creating amazing friction. Fucking couples surrounded me, but all I could focus on were his cocks deep inside of me. Every thrust sparked pleasure inside of me, making sounds come from my throat.

"Ezra," I sighed his name in pleasure.

My pussy clenched around him, earning a strangled groan from Ezra. He knew I needed more to be able to come, and his tail flicked over my clit again. Pleasure rose inside of me as his cocks fucked me hard and his tail pleasured my clit.

My climax was building steadily, and I knew it wouldn't be long before it would take over my body. Ezra knew my body almost better than I did, and he increased his thrusts, trying to get me to that high. His tail circled my clit slowly, applying pressure to it until I burst. A scream of pleasure tore from my throat as my orgasm ripped through me. My pussy and ass squeezed around his cock as my body trembled with pleasure.

Ezra hissed when I milked his cocks, suddenly losing his own fight. His cocks throbbed and spurted inside of me, filling me with his cum, only enhancing my orgasm. Pleasure washed over me as my body spasmed and moans left me.

My legs gave out, but Ezra held me steady as he filled me with his release. When the last of his cum trickled out of my holes, he pulled back. Hissing as he saw how much he had filled me.

"Beautiful," he murmured as he pushed his cum back inside of me.

I sighed as I let my body fall on the towel, too far gone to care that my legs were wide open and everyone could see me filled with his cum. Ezra's gentle caresses made me come back down from my high slowly.

When I felt like I could breathe again, he kissed me.

"Ready for a swim?" Ezra asked.

I laughed and followed him into the cool water, which felt amazing on my overheated skin.

This vacation turned out to be the best one I had ever had, and I couldn't wait to go back with Ezra. The best part besides all the amazing sex, was that I went home with no tan lines.

THE END

Authors Note

I cannot believe this is already part 5 of my creature loving collection and the fifth part of my amazing bonus couple!

I really hope I can continue this collection and that my bonus character has so many more stories to share!

Have you seen the character art I had created of Ezra and the delicious NSFW art? You can see both pieces on my website and purchase them in my Etsy Shop!

https://lilithleana.wordpress.com/ezra-the-naga-character-and-nsfw-art/

I also had character art created for my Gargoyle Théo, my Satyr Sylas and my lovely Yetis!

Anyway, I hope you enjoyed the story! Please leave a rating and/or a review if you did.

About the author

Lilith Leana writes what she loves; Monster, fantasy, and sci-fi erotica.

Born and raised in Belgium, she devours ebooks as if it heals her. In her day job she loves to organize, plan and make schedules for other people, but when the night falls she can let loose with her fantasies which star all kinds of Monsters and Human couplings.

YOU CAN ALSO FIND ME on:

New Author Website: https://lilithleana.wordpress.com/

New Newsletter! Sign Up to be kept up to date about my new releases, sales, character art, and giveaways: Sign Up Form[1]

Instagram: https://www.instagram.com/lilithleana/

Etsy Shop: https://www.etsy.com/be/shop/SteamyPublishing

Or you can email me: lilith.leana666@gmail.com

DEAR READER

If you enjoyed this book, please consider leaving a review. Indie writers depend on reviews to keep writing and publishing.

Thank you so much ❤

Lilith

---

1.   https://dashboard.mailerlite.com/forms/533589/95138330138642151/share

Also by the author

Series & Collections

<u>Creature Loving Volume 1: A Monster Erotica Collection</u>[1]
<u>Creature Loving Volume 2: A Monster Erotica Collection</u>[2]
<u>Creature Loving Volume 3: A Monster Erotica Collection</u>[3]
<u>Creature Loving Volume 4: A Monster Erotica Collection</u>[4]
<u>Creature Loving Holidays 1: A Monster Erotica Collection</u>[5]
<u>Grim Lovers 1: An Erotic Fairytale Collection</u>[6]
<u>Grim Lovers 2: An Erotic Fairytale Collection</u>[7]
<u>My Ghostly Lover</u>[8]
<u>My Orc Mate</u>[9]

---

1. https://books2read.com/u/47gLkj

2. https://books2read.com/u/47VMwA

3. https://books2read.com/u/bW0pk1

4. https://books2read.com/u/3LxQD1

5. https://books2read.com/u/bp6Yyg

6. https://books2read.com/u/4AA7Zp

7. https://books2read.com/u/mZpjNe

8. https://books2read.com/u/3J6dxJ

9. https://books2read.com/u/3yd90L

Sneak Peak of my Next Story:
Nesting with the Shifter

"*Happy, my Mate?*" *Kai asked as he slowly ground his cock against me. I moaned as my pussy squeezed around nothing, achingly empty and so ready to have him inside of me. "I would be happier if you would fuck me," I moaned, biting my lip as I realized how forward I was being.*

I wasn't even in heat yet and I still craved his cock more than I needed my next breath. My nest was ready and my body was, too. It was time to complete our mating bond.

"So needy," Kai purred. "Do you need my cock in your pussy?"

I gasped at his crude words, but the wetness seeping out of my pussy showed how much I loved it. "Yes, please," I moaned.

He opened my legs wider and pushed me lower on the nest. My nose was in the bear's fur he had brought and I loved that it smelled like him.

"So pretty, and tight," he purred as he let his finger tease the opening of my pussy. "You think you can take all of me?" he asked.

"Yes, give it to me," I moaned, my hands gripping tightly in the fur as I arched my back to push my backside closer to him.

"I need to take care of my Mate," he said as he let one finger sink in my pussy. "But first, I need another taste."

His mouth made contact with my pussy and a low, throaty sound of pleasure came from me. His tongue felt amazing against my oversensitive flesh. So very different from that of a Wolf, but oh so good. I wondered if there were other differences between us. We had our whole lives to discover each other bodies and minds, learning the differences and the ways we fit together.

I loved his tongue on me, but I craved his cock deep inside of me. "Please, Kai," I moaned, my pussy clenching around nothing. "I need you inside."

"Anything for you, Vanya," he said as he positioned his cock head at my entrance.

I bit back a whimper and the urge to beg him for more. He pushed in slowly, breathing heavily as if trying to contain himself, but I didn't want to slow. I wanted him to ravish me, take me like a Mate should take his beloved and ruin me for any other men.

"More," I moaned as I pushed my ass closer to him, gaining another inch of his cock.

"I love to hear you beg, but I can't resist the tight clasp of your pussy," Kai groaned as he pushed in further.

Oh so slowly, he gave me inch after delicious inch of his cock, stretching me to the edge of my comfort zone. But I was made for my Mate and he was made for me so we fit perfectly. A deep moan came from me as he bottomed out, filling me with his amazing cock. He touched every pleasure spot inside of me, sparking pleasure with every move.

"Fuck, you feel amazing, Vanya," he purred as he slowly pulled out and pushed back in.

"Oh, Goddess yes," I moaned as more pleasure filled me.

Nesting with the Shifter - Coming Soon - 30 March